A sad princess sat at her castle window.
She had never laughed and didn't even
know how to. Her mom and dad didn't think
anybody could make their daughter smile.
Until one day along came. . .

For Zoë, Katy, and Philippa

Published in the United States 1986 by
Dial Books for Young Readers
A Division of E. P. Dutton
A Division of New American Library
2 Park Avenue, New York, New York 10016

Published in Canada by Fitzhenry & Whiteside, Toronto
First published in Great Britain by Andersen Press
Copyright © 1985 by Tony Ross
All rights reserved
Printed in Italy
First Edition
COBE
2 4 6 8 10 9 7 5 3 1

Library of Congress Cataloging in Publication Data
Ross, Tony. Lazy Jack.
Summary: A lazy, dim-witted boy who can never do anything right
makes a sad princess laugh, thereby winning her hand.
[1. Fairy tales. 2. Folklore — England.] I. Title.
PZ8.R668Laz 1986 398.2'2'0941 [E] 85-16180
ISBN 0-8037-0275-2

*The art for each picture consists of a black ink
and watercolor painting, which is camera-separated
and reproduced in full color.*

LAZY JACK

TONY ROSS

Dial Books for Young Readers
New York

Once upon a time there was a boy called Jack who lived with his mother. Jack was probably the laziest person in the whole world. He would just sit around while his mother did all the work.

Finally Jack's mother couldn't take any more of his
laziness.

"Go out and get a job," she shouted. "Otherwise
you'll get no more meals from me! And you'll have to
wash your own socks too."

"Okay," said Jack, and he went to work for a farmer
who paid him a shiny gold coin for a day's work.

On the way home Jack had to jump over a stream, and he dropped the gold coin into the water.

Of course his mother was angry.

"Dodo!" she cried. "You should have put it in your jacket pocket."

"Okay," said Jack. "Next time I will."

The next day Jack went to work for a cow keeper who paid him with a jug of milk.

Remembering his mother's advice, he poured the milk into his pocket and went home.

"Nincompoop!" shouted his mother. "You should have carried the jug on your head."

"Okay," said Jack. "Next time I will."

Next Jack went to work at a dairy. As his pay he was given a fine cheese.

Remembering his mother's advice, he put the cheese on
his head. By the time he got home, it had melted into
a gooey mess.

"Feather-brained airhead!" screeched his mother.
"You should have carried it in your arms."

"Okay," said Jack. "Next time I will."

Jack's next job was in a hot dog factory where he was given a cat as his pay.

Remembering his mother's advice, he carried the cat home in his arms.

The cat was a nasty creature who hated being picked up.

When Jack got home, he was scratched all over.
   "Bubble-headed flea brain!" yelled his mother.
   "You should have dragged it behind you on a string."
   "Okay," said Jack. "Next time I will."
   The next day he went to work in a bakery.

The bakers were pleased with Jack's work, and they paid him with a cake.

Remembering his mother's advice, Jack dragged it home behind him on a string.

"Nitwitted pinhead!" shouted his mother. "You should have carried it on your back."

"Okay," said Jack. "Next time I will."
Next Jack went to work in a stable.

When the work was finished, the owner of the stable gave Jack a donkey as payment.

Remembering his mother's advice, Jack heaved the donkey onto his back.

It was not easy, not easy at all, and Jack staggered away toward home.

On his way he passed the castle of the sad princess who had never laughed, and she happened to be sitting at her window.

She watched Jack stagger by with his donkey on his back.

He looked so funny . . .

that the sad princess burst out laughing.

The princess's mom and dad were so happy, they let Jack marry her.

The princess was happy to have such a funny husband.

And Jack was happiest of all because he never had to work again.